This story is dedicated to all the men and women who lost their lives while fishing the sea, including Rocky's brother Lorry Gaudet.
ALC

To you, strong-willed child, you know what color makes you vibrate, you listen to your heart and follow your path . . .
MD

We gratefully acknowledge for their financial support of our publishing program the Canada Council for the Arts, the Ontario Arts Council and the Government of Canada.

Library and Archives Canada Cataloguing in Publication
Title: Rocky waters / Anne Laurel Carter ; [illustrated by] Marianne Dumas.
Names: Carter, Anne, author. | Dumas, Marianne, illustrator.
Identifiers: Canadiana (print) 20189067314 | Canadiana (ebook) 20189067322 | ISBN 9781773060972 (hardcover) | ISBN 9781773060989 (EPUB) | ISBN 9781773062815 (Kindle)
Classification: LCC PS8555.A7727 R63 2019 | DDC jC813/.54—dc23

The illustrations are in watercolor.
Design by Michael Solomon
Printed and bound in Malaysia

MIX
Paper from
responsible sources
FSC® C012700
www.fsc.org

Canada Council
for the Arts

Conseil des Arts
du Canada

ONTARIO ARTS COUNCIL
CONSEIL DES ARTS DE L'ONTARIO
an Ontario government agency
un organisme du gouvernement de l'Ontario

With the participation of the Government of Canada
Avec la participation du gouvernement du Canada

Canadä

ROCKY WATERS

Anne Laurel Carter

PICTURES BY

Marianne Dumas

GROUNDWOOD BOOKS
HOUSE OF ANANSI PRESS
TORONTO   BERKELEY

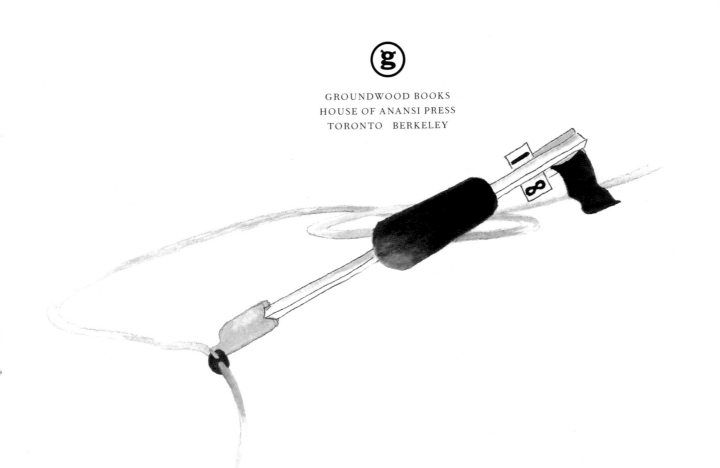

In a small house, on a small island by the sea . . .

Rocky sleeps beside his six older brothers, his six older sisters across the hall, and dreams he's fishing with his ancestors.

At 4:00 a.m. Mum taps the kitchen ceiling. "Anyone going fishing?"

Rocky runs downstairs. "Lobster season! Can I come?"

"Do any of those boots fit you?" Dad asks.

Rocky slips his feet into the smallest pair of fishing boots at the back door, clomps around the kitchen and trips over the mat.

"Not yet," Dad says. "One day soon."

But soon doesn't come. School does.

All day, every day, his teacher's voice scratches and the walls squeeze. Rocky stares out the window.

Dories and Northumberland-style boats sail across the sea-blue sky. His ancestors invite him to go fishing. *À la pêche!*

Every day after school, Rocky meets Dad and his older sister Patsy at the wharf. "How many pounds did you catch today?"

"Seven hundred," says Dad.

"School's not for me," Rocky says. "I want to learn fishing."

"If the salt's still in your veins when you're Patsy's age, you can leave school and fish all you want."

Rodney Rocky G.

CHARLOTTETOWN, P.E.I.

All winter, Rocky helps Dad make lobster traps.

Spring finally arrives, and with it a new lobster season.

Rocky can hardly sleep. He hears Mum's tap and runs downstairs. Dad and Patsy are already at the breakfast table.

"Can I come fishing?"

"Try on some boots," Dad says. "They might fit you this year."

Rocky slips on the smallest pair and walks around the kitchen, careful to avoid the mat.

"I'm ready!" Rocky pulls something out of his pocket. "I've got my own boat!"

Mum hands him a bowl of hot porridge. "Eat up so you don't get seasick."

At the wharf, Rocky and Patsy undo the lines and jump on board.

The sky is still dark. Harbor lights wink as they sail out. The sea's voice swells with adventure. There are no walls, only the sun on the rise.

Rocky feels as free as a seagull.

They pass other fishing boats. Everyone waves.

At the helm, Dad stops at their first buoy and reminds Rocky how he lost three fingers in a winch when he was younger.

"So you stay out of the way when I haul the traps on the winch. And mind the ropes on deck when we dump 'em. Those ropes can grab your foot and take you overboard, and your mother expects you home for supper."

Dad hauls up the first line of traps. Patsy measures each lobster, tossing babies and pregnant mothers back into the water. She puts rubber bands around the claws of the big ones.

"Can I try?" Rocky asks.

"Careful! The pincher hurts if it gets you."

Rocky holds the bander and tries.

"Ow!" he screams. "It got me!"

Patsy blows air on the claw to make it close up tight, and Rocky bands it.

Soon they work faster as a team. Patsy holds the claws and Rocky bands. He counts the market lobsters in each haul so Dad can mark the best spots on his map.

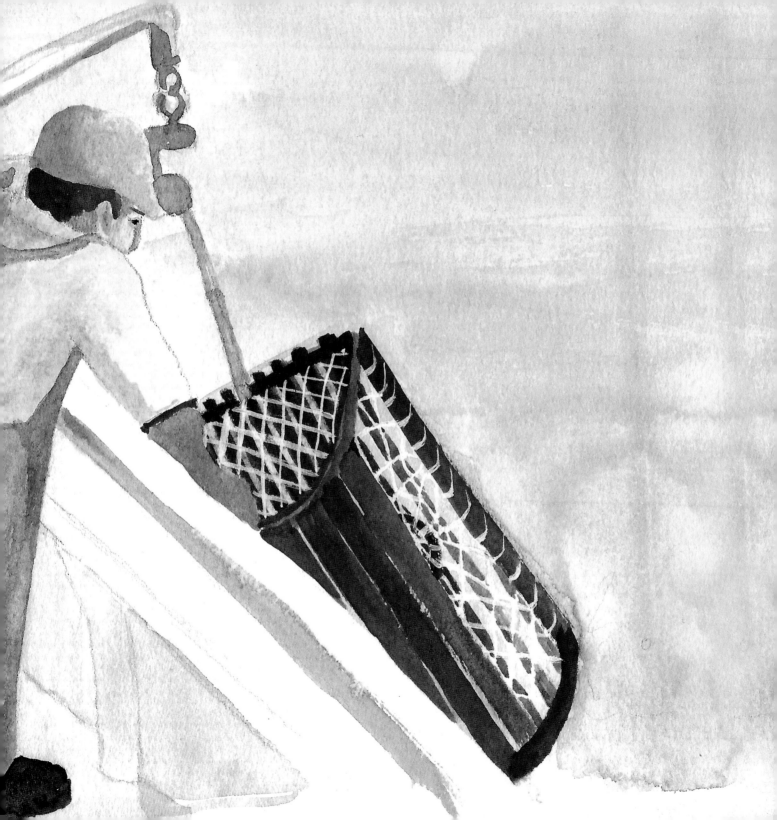

Patsy places four small mackerel inside each trap as bait.

"Stand back, Rocky," Dad says and helps Patsy push the traps along the washboard. They lay the rope in tidy coils on the deck so their feet won't get caught in it.

As Dad drives the boat, Patsy shoves each trap overboard. *Plunk!* The rope whips out as the traps sink to the bottom of the sea.

It takes all day to empty and re-set three hundred traps —
thirty lines with ten traps each.

Finally, Dad says, "There's the one we're looking for!"

When the last traps are emptied and lined up ready on the
washboard, Patsy shoves them back into the sea.

Dad smiles at Rocky. "Time to sail home."

Rocky sulks. "I wish we could stay out and fish again tomorrow."

"No fishing allowed on Sundays," Dad laughs. "You've got the salt bad in your veins. I'll bring you out every Saturday as long as there's no storm."

Rocky plays with his boat. Patsy starts to clean the deck,
but Dad needs a nap in the cuddy so she takes the helm.

"I can steer," Rocky offers. He
climbs up on the captain's chair.
Patsy points at the lighthouse in
the distance. "Just hold her steady. No
whistling, remember. It's bad luck."

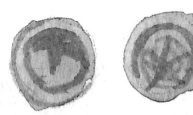

Rocky remembers not to whistle but watching the shore gets boring. Where did he leave *his* boat?

He sees it on the washboard and jumps down to get it. He wishes he could sail it out and keep fishing.

"We're going in a circle!" Patsy laughs and grabs the helm. "Why did you leave?"

"I didn't want my boat to go overboard," Rocky says. "Don't tell Dad."

At the wharf, the lobsters are weighed.
"A good catch today," Dad says and
gives Rocky a dollar. "You were a big help."

Patsy grins, keeping Rocky's secret. "Are
you saving up for anything?"

"My own boat," he says. "I'll name it
Rocky Waters."

Rocky falls asleep at the dinner table and dreams
he's old enough to fish the sea — a world where
there are no walls, and he feels free.

Author's Note

In 1799, eight Acadian families landed on a windswept tip of Prince Edward Island and decided to settle there. Rocky's ancestors — the Gaudets — were one of those founding families. They honored the place with a Mi'kmaq name — Tignish (meaning *paddle*) — and became fishermen.

This story is set in the 1970s and is inspired by Rocky's stories about his childhood. Rocky quit school as a young teenager to live his dream. At nineteen, he was diagnosed with leukemia. Two things saved his life. His sister Patsy generously donated her bone marrow for his treatment, and Rocky was determined to return to the world he loved — the sea. Rocky continues to fish for lobster in Tignish in the late spring and in Riverport, Nova Scotia, during the winter season.

Glossary

À la pêche – Let's go fishing.

bander – A small tool for fitting a rubber band around a lobster's claws.

buoy – A floating device.

cuddy – A small room on a boat.

dory, dories (pl.) – A small traditional fishing boat with high sides and a flat bottom.

helm – The tiller or wheel for steering a boat.

Northumberland-style boat – A fishing boat with a sharp bow and flared hull that help drive spray away from the deck, designed for the choppy seas around the Northumberland Strait in Canada's Gulf of St. Lawrence.

washboard – A wooden plank fixed to the upper part of a boat's side that helps keep out the spray and sea.

winch – A device used to lift or pull, consisting of a rope, cable or chain that is wound around a drum and turned by a motor or crank.